About the Author

Suganthi Mahadevan Shivkumar is an aspiring writer from Singapore. Born and raised in the tiny red dot, she was raised by an English teacher mother, who from an early age, inspired her to read, write and speak fluent English and write elegant stories and poetry. Despite a hectic life as a female corporate executive, Suganthi has always nurtured her love for writing and often finds this to be a very effective and natural way to detox from a stressful day. She particularly loves to write about real life events, people and things that touch our daily lives and leave an indelible mark. A hugely positive and forward looking person who loves inspirational quotes, stories and generally simply being happy, she is a doting mother of two teenagers, a devoted wife to a very supportive husband and his loving parents, and a close sibling to her elder sister and a dear and trusted friend to many. Suganthi who was raised by her strong willed mum who was widowed at a very early age after just five years of marriage, raised her and her elder sister single-handedly in tough circumstances. Suganthi continues to draw daily determination and strength from the everlasting teachings and life of her beloved late mother, to whom this first piece of work is totally dedicated.

Dedication

My first book is entirely dedicated to my beloved late mother and mentor, Saroja Mahadevan, who was simply unconditional love personified. She taught me to love the English language and nurtured the keen passion to read and write from a very early age. She herself was a prolific writer of sorts and wrote inspirational letters to her dearest grandchildren. My first book is a small tribute to her love for everyone's children, her passion for writing, her unconditional affection, support and extended hand to all in need and her untiring positivity in the toughest situations. She taught my sister and me to have faith that The Creator never closes all doors on anyone. He may shut one but opens many others. Truly, she lived her entire life celebrating the gift of life, love and hope. This story is about the gift of life, the blessings we receive and celebrating life as seen through the eyes of a pet dog.

I must surely thank my beloved family, husband, Shivkumar, parents-in-law, Kamala and Muthukrishnan, who are really my parents too, my lovely daughters, Maanasa and Aarthi, sister, Jayanthi, brother-in-law, Ravi, nephew, Vinod for their encouragement and support through this adventure. Very importantly, I thank my pet dog, Theo, for the inspiration he has been and continues to be to us all. To a large extent, I imagine these stories as I gaze into his innocent eyes, thinking these may be the thoughts fleeting through his mind. This story attempts to give Theo the voice he does not have and yet so effectively communicates with his kindness, love and gratitude. Perhaps he is fortunate not to have a tongue that speaks – he sees and experiences the world through us this way.

My sincere thanks to Krish Datta and his family for nurturing the canine friendships between their Spot and our Theo as this gives us delightful stories in themselves.

Finally, I must thank Uma Jeyaram and her lovely daughter Vandhana Jeyaram for the excitement and effort they demonstrated in providing illustrations so my story could visually speak in this book.

A big thank you to all my closest friends who knew of my aspiration and supported me in silent ways as well.

Suganthi Mahadevan
Shivkumar

EVERY DOG HAS HIS DAY!

Illustrated by Vandhana Jeyaram

AUSTIN MACAULEY
PUBLISHERS LTD.

A CIP catalogue record for this title is available from the British Library.

ISBN 9781785549465 (Paperback)
ISBN 9781785549472 (Hardback)
ISBN 9781785549489 (E-Book)

www.austinmacauley.com

First Published (2016)
Austin Macauley Publishers Ltd.
25 Canada Square
Canary Wharf
London
E14 5LQ

Acknowledgements

My mother, Saroja Mahadevan, who will forever remain my strongest role model, my supportive husband, Shivkumar, beloved daughters, Maanasa and Aarthi and of course our most loved and loving pet dog, Theo, a soul deeply connected to our family in this journey to show us and teach us what unconditional love is all about.

Chapter 1

From the Pet Farm to the Pet Store

I have been snuggled up in my small enclosure all day and night since I arrived at the Happy Pets Store three days ago. The store name suggested that I should be happy and joyous but I felt very confined and claustrophobic. I was much freer in the dog farm. No one seemed to care that I hardly had any room to move around. Fortunately I was petite and small – others called me cute, a term I did not really understand or bother about. I was beginning to feel really sad and lonely.

I could tell I was not alone. Like me, there were some thirty other puppies in individual cages. We were stacked next to one another. Hmmmmmm... I shall never make a friend here, I thought to myself melancholically.

Fear gripped me for the first time – what was I fearful of? Well, I really did not know. I could feel a pit in my tummy and a painful lump in my throat ever since I came to this store. Many questions inundated my mind. Why could I not just stay with my mummy and siblings at the farm? Why was I here? Why was I not free? So many questions flooded my mind. Yet I had no clue or any answers.

Then on the fourth day, I was bathed and dried, nails clipped and my matted fur brushed silky smooth! I could feel some change was happening but could not understand what this was all about. I decided that I should just await and enjoy the changes, as I really did not have any control over them anyway!

I sensed that James, the pet store assistant, was fond of me after he groomed me so well.

He kept carrying me around like a handbag slung over his forearm that day as he expressively flaunted; "Look at my most adorable Shih Tzu! He has the perfect, lustrous coat of white and golden brown, expressive eyes, fluffy ears, the cutest face that can melt your heart and above all, a very even temperament unlike most of his species!"

He kept patting my head and scratching me behind my ears as he repeated his praises again and again! Whatever he meant, I felt good for the first time in this store. I felt he was kind and started to like him too.

So I started making my first human friend in James! In the meantime, he introduced me to a beagle that he had just groomed. He put us both in a common larger play area to see how we got along. The beagle sniffed me all over incessantly in his true signature beagle style! We played and got along quite well. This beagle was my first canine friend here! Two new friendships in a day was really an awesome blessing for me and I was truly thankful for the changes that day four at the store brought into my life!

I was happy for the friendships and felt positive about the changes. For the first time, I slept peacefully that night. I was actually looking forward to more action the next day and strongly felt that good things would start to happen.

Chapter 2

Going Home with My New Family

As I woke up, I found several pairs of eyes peering into my enclosure and excitedly exclaiming, "This one looks amazingly cute and adorable! Please let us have a closer look at him!"

James was very proud to display me to these people who had walked into the store. They had seen several other puppies and were about to leave when the lady amongst them spotted me!

The two girls were very charmed by my energy and good looks and kept persuading their mummy to take me back with them. Mummy liked me but was a little hesitant about making a sudden impulsive decision.

She kept telling her two daughters, "This puppy is very adorable I agree. However, do you realise that you are making a very significant decision here? We shall be responsible for him for the rest of his life. We have to take care of his every need like a baby. There is no turning back on this decision. He may get old and sick and even so, we must love him with all our heart and take even better care of him then. This is truly a lifetime commitment."

The girls said an emphatic yes to everything and as Daddy walked in, persuaded him too. Daddy was easily persuaded and then James started gathering all the paraphernalia they would need as they took me home. It was a long list including a doggie bag, a play pen, a fencing for the play pen, a tray for my biological needs, some treats, doggie shampoo, conditioner, fur brush, harness and leash, water and food containers, and vitamins for starters. Mummy listened intently to every instruction James uttered and asked many questions. The two girls were immensely thankful to their parents and excited to take me back with them.

Once again, I knew this meant change for me! I felt sad to leave James and my beagle friend whom I had started to bond with. Yet I somehow felt that this next change was going to be positive and reassuring. I wagged my tail and bid farewell to my two friends as I was carried out by Mummy surrounded by her cheerful family, who were now adopting me.

I was comfortably taken to their three-storey home in a very stable car ride with the doting family around me, who praised and patted me non-stop. I felt loved, I must say, and it felt good to be with them. Once again, I had my set of questions but no answers. I decided to go with the flow, as just like before, I really had no options. My instincts told me this would be a good change, and I wanted to believe my inner voice.

My new family was as helpless as I was once they took me back. "Where will he sleep? What shall we call him? Can he come inside our bedrooms? Do we keep him on a leash? Will he feel awkward with the change of place?" they piled question after question.

Mummy was overwhelmed but I could tell she was in charge and I felt safe in her hands. She carried me like a baby while the rest of the family set up my playpen, surrounding frame, poo tray, water bottle and some treats. As she put me down I crumpled all the newspaper and made several concentric circles and lay down. They all seemed humoured by my natural actions. I barked a lot that first day with them.

Daddy was very happy he finally had male company in his family as the females outnumbered him! So I knew I was immediately taken as their son - a follicularly endowed son with four legs, canines and a fluffy tail!

8

Chapter 3

Getting a Name and Becoming Family

While I sat in my playpen, Megan, the elder daughter, rattled off some possible names for me – Prince, Cookie, and Castle were top on her list. It was like a competition as Angel, her younger sister, then listed more including Twinkle, Star and Hero. They repeated these to me expecting some reaction, which I was really not sure of. Every name was discarded due to my lack of reaction, they commented.

Hmmmmmm, this was way too complicated for me, so I just rested and crumpled more newspaper, relieved myself and just slept over my poo and pee!

Megan and Angel were extremely upset by my latest actions and orchestrated a "Yucky! Mummy, he just slept over his own mess!"

I liked Mummy's reaction. She seemed to understand this was normal for me! She punctuated that understanding with, "We shall need to train him dearies! And on his name, since we are agreeing to disagree on all the suggestions, why don't we call him Theo? After all, it was our old neighbour's dog Theo who inspired you to get a dog. That shall be a good memory of our good old friend Theo too."

Mummy got everyone to agree at the speed of lightning and so I was named Theo! Everyone took turns to call me Theo in different tones; it was a musical experience for me!

Mummy patted my head calling out, "Theo Baby!" before cleaning me up and laying new sheets and putting me down again. She seemed to exude so much love in her touch, smile, words and actions that I must say she was the first I loved almost immediately. She was strict and firm but warm and affectionate. She handled me with tender love and explained everything patiently to her daughters and family. I gathered from their discussions that only Mummy had had a pet dog previously. That explained why I felt most secure and safe in her hands!

The very next day, they made a signboard that read 'THEO' with paw marks and displayed that in my playpen. The first month was a period of learning, relearning, adjustments and settling in. Each day, I was allowed to venture more and more into the interiors of our home. I felt they started trusting me and me them. There was a bond and sense of belonging that I felt like never before.

Occasionally, I earned the wrath of my family by messing up. This happened when I crumpled newspaper as soon as they laid them, bit shoe laces or footwear that they left at the shoe rack outside the main entrance, dug deep holes in the little garden they had and made paw prints on the walkway and hallway as I ran in! Being locked up outside or being confined to my playpen as punishment, I began to understand that this meant I should not do these things. My family drew up the list of dos and don'ts.

I must say the latter seemed to be longer than the former. The best part was I got rewarded every time I did well too. That helped me do more good than bad! They also taught me to shake hands, roll over, stand and parade on my hind legs and fetch toys! I was as proud of my talents as they seemed to be. Whenever friends visited, my family would especially make me do these tricks as they called them and of course reward me with tasty treats.

My family doted on me. With every passing day, I grew closer to them. They took me to the nearby parks each day where I could socialise with other dogs. My sisters would go to school each morning and Mummy and Daddy to work. I would have the entire house to myself. They had a stay-in domestic helper and this aunty was very kind to me too. She fed me, slowly learned to shower me and played with me. I looked forward to the reunion with my family each evening and felt very sad when Mummy or Daddy had to travel on work matters.

I could tell when luggage was ready that someone was leaving and I would sit on the packed bags as a sign of protest! This used to earn me some bonus pats and praises, as they too would feel sad to leave me. They said I had a very high IQ! Little did I understand this but it seemed I was sensitive to happenings in their lives. Likewise, when someone in the family fell ill, I would stay by their bedside wishing I could help. This would bring a broad smile to their faces and I loved that! Overall, this was my beloved family and looking back, I was so grateful that they adopted me.

Days, weeks, months and years passed by. There were good days, average days and great days! I was groomed beautifully, fed like a king, looked after like a baby and my life was perfect! I often thought about my other beagle friend and acquaintances in the pet store and hoped they too had found good homes like me.

Chapter 4

Overcoming My First Fear

Actually, very honestly, my family had helped me overcome my greatest insecurity and fear! Deep inside, I was so fearful of being abandoned, or having no friends or no one to care for me. My family had shown me, through sheer love and care, that they were with me all the way, through every change. I felt so secure and safe with them in what I began to call my home!

I had extended family too. My sisters' uncle, aunt, cousin and grandparents all treated me as their own too. They would miss me and come visit me as often as they could. Like my sisters, I received gifts on special occasions too! My birthday was marked on their calendars and yes, my name was even passwords on some of their devices! Shhhhh! This is a secret of course! I specifically liked posing for the flattering pictures that my sisters' favourite cousin brother, Vincent, took of me. He posted them on social media and wrote such complimentary narratives of me. They always made me feel special and very well loved!

My birthdays were special. My family decorated the home with party banners and balloons, ordered lovely cakes and even invited close family and friends. On my third birthday, I was pleasantly surprised that one of our closest family friends brought a surprise guest to my birthday party!

"Sniff! Sniff! Sniff!" the guest appeared.

It was a beagle they had just adopted! He was just like the first, the only canine friend I had made in the pet store three years ago! He was like a brother from another mother and we hit it off from that day!

Macaroon, as he was named, was a friendly beagle, a little oddly sized, which really added to his cuteness. He became a regular visitor to our place and likewise I eventually had a second home in his. Macaroon and I enjoyed our staycations in each other's homes when our immediate families went on their vacations. We never had to stay with strangers or in doggie motels – phew! Again, it was reinforcement that my family would never abandon me and that I had a second home too!

I was blessed with a family that took me to the best veterinary clinic in town when I was a little under the weather or needed immunisation and check-ups, the best groomer for keeping my furry coat neat and lustrous.

Doggie Spa Treatment

Once in a while I even had a doggie spa treatment at the groomers! What else could I even pray for except that my family and I would always be together and close. Even as I slept each night, the voices of my family fondly calling out to me, "Theo, Theo Baby," reverberated in my head!

Much as I grew on them and them on me, I developed two other major fears, for which I needed the support of my family to overcome. I displayed these fears quite visibly, hoping my family would help me cope with each.

Chapter 5

Overcoming My Second Fear

I had developed a chilling fear of downpours, lightning and thunder! The claps of thunder, flashes of light and heavy downpours sent chills through my spine. I would run helter-skelter and look for shelter. Nothing would soothe me as I felt the world was crashing down on me. I would helplessly climb onto the dining table, and bark for attention. I would run up to find a hiding spot in the bedrooms and would climb into open shelves only to jump out at the next rumbling thunder or flash of bright light! Mummy tried diverting my attention with my favourite treats.

Fear paralysed every taste bud and I would not even be tempted to taste the treat! Mummy, Megan and Angel would huddle around me and comfort me by stroking me and talking to me. My tail drooping down, my body trembling, I would hardly be soothed.

Then one day, Mummy had a brilliant idea. She discussed it with Megan and Angel and they all seemed very excited. In the interim, they continued to make me pose for pictures, an activity I had enjoyed from a young age. They dressed me up, made me sport shades, caps, T-shirts and all sorts of accessories and took beautiful pictures of me, many of which became prominent displays in the living room, dining room and bedrooms and as screensavers on their mobile devices.

The next day, there was a torrential downpour and I was in my usual fearful mood. Megan dressed me up, Angel adorned me with beautiful accessories and Mummy carried me. We all walked to the sheltered balcony on the second floor camera in hand as if to take pictures.

There, with every flash of lightning and clap of thunder, Megan and Angel would smile looking up into the bright sky exclaiming, "Mummy, we don't need the camera. See God is taking our pictures. We need to smile!" And all of them would smile the brightest, sunniest smile ever and look at me and urge me to smile along saying, "Theo, God is taking your picture and you must smile and look good!"

It must have been their loving convincing act or some magical affection, I started believing that God was taking my picture from above and the flashes of light illuminated the dark skies to give clarity to the pictures and the claps of thunder were the shutters of God's heavenly, heavy duty camera taking a high resolution picture from oh so far, far away! This ritual was repeated with every rain over the next month and I was surely getting over my useless fear of downpours!

Once again, my supportive family had helped me out and I was eternally thankful. I realised how useless feeling fear was. Instead, my family taught me to accept and overcome it and that life was really simple, we complicate it with unfounded fears and thoughts!

Now that I had overcome my second fear, I grew confident that I could tide over my third fear too. All I had to do was to work with my family and trust them to help me. I was ready to do just that.

Chapter 6

Overcoming My Final Fear

I had a bizarre fear of motorcycles and scooters. Their engines just drove me wild and crazy. They triggered a frenzy in me and I would start barking unstoppably whenever they came close or started revving their engines. You can imagine I would bark wildly at every postman, pizza delivery man, newspaper vendor and just about every motorcycle that whizzed past our home or when I was out walking. I would lose my mind trying to camouflage my fear with shrill and loud barks. This annoyed my family, neighbours and the riders. Everyone grossly misunderstood me as not liking them. This was far from true – I was actually phobic of the two and three wheelers after an incident in my early days with my family. I vividly recall the incident with a pizza delivery man. He had just arrived at our home to deliver pizza to my sisters and their friends. With four pizza boxes stacked one above the other, he got off his motorcycle and was about to walk straight in through the open gate. Naturally my canine instincts kicked in and I wanted to ensure this stranger was security cleared to enter. I ran up to him and acted like the fiercest dog in the world. I barked very loudly and sprung up at him to compensate for my lacking height as if to show I was no pushover! Little did I realise I might have overdone my act! The pizza delivery man ran in concentric circles around his parked motorcycle with the boxes precariously perched on his hands outstretched above his head! As he ran, I chased him round and round, barking!

He dropped box after box as he ran screaming! It was all at the speed of lightning that my family could neither calm him nor me. He was furious with me and wanted to teach me a lesson. I thought we were both just having some fun till this devious delivery man stepped back into his seat, started his machine and ran his rear wheel over my tail and hind leg.

"Oooooouchhhhh!" it hurt so much and I could not take the excruciating pain he had inflicted on me. My dear family rushed me to the veterinary clinic for immediate treatment of my wounds, which were fortunately not too serious despite the bleeding and pain! I also got a lecture on my over-acting and its consequences. I listened with my head down, as I was also ashamed of what I had done.

Mummy and Daddy also lodged official complaints about the irresponsible and cruel pizza delivery man so he did not keep hurting animals deliberately. Nonetheless, this incident had left an indelible mark on me and I developed an immediate fear of motorcycles and scooters, imagining they were all capable of hurting me in this manner!

I started developing a fear of bicycles as well. Basically, the circulation of large wheels and the sound of the engine triggered an inexplicable fear in me. I would tremble and bark loudly and start chasing my own tail running in circles, all the while biting my fluffy tail till it often bled! My family would try to grab me and stop me but I would keep running in fast circles until I got completely exhausted and would then just lie on the ground with a wet tail that was frequently stained with blood!

I did not like the aftermath of this and I knew my family too was not delighted to see this obsessive-compulsive disorder of mine!

Daddy devised a clever plan, discussed this with my family and with their support, he was very sure they would help me overcome my fear and these unproductive outcomes. Megan and Angel bought fancy carriers for their bicycles. They dressed the carriers up with cushions and placed me in the little dog carrier while cycling in my favourite park close to home. I was surely nervous at first but soon with every passing day, I was distracted and started enjoying the rides and breeze. Slowly they lowered the carrier to a position just above the rear wheel. I could hear and see the bicycle wheel but felt safe and secure in my carrier and soon got used to the rotating wheel beneath me!

Daddy exclaimed by the end of his two-week trial; "See, I knew I could kill two birds with one stone! Megan and Angel are finally riding their bicycles regularly, and most importantly, Theo is now over his fear of bicycles and rotating wheels! Theo was clearly afraid of the unknown. Once he experienced the positives like enjoying a joy ride and the breeze in the park, he realised he uselessly feared the unknown! Now, he can focus on the positives and let go of his fear!"

Again, I had learned that my fear was unfounded and really based on what I was unaware of.

Now that I had passed the bicycle stage, Daddy's next challenge was to get me used to motorcycles and the like. So, he transferred the dog carrier onto our neighbour's motorcycle and started the machine! My heart skipped several beats and I started barking in fear. He turned it off and started to calm me down. He took me back on the bicycle to make sure I was still comfortable and I was. This ritual was repeated every evening over the next four weeks and my tolerance grew better each day. I was soon able to ride this machine that stirred the worst fears in me! It felt even better than the bicycle as we moved faster. Daddy certainly restricted the rides to around our neighbourhood only so we did not flout traffic rules in any way.

I was finally able to let go of this fear that had gripped me for such a long time!

"Thank you Daddy!" I said with lots of gratitude in my heart. I was so thankful that I had the best family in the world. They supported me in such small but important ways. They never gave up when I seemed impossible. They kept encouraging me and believed that I could surely overcome my fears.

This made me believe in myself even more. I did this for myself for sure but even more because I could not let my family down. A major milestone in my life! From that day onwards, I was wagging my tail and barking friendly barks at the postman, pizza delivery man, and all riders. I did not hurt myself either. It was such a pleasant change all round!

Chapter 7

Reciprocating Care to My Family

I felt very indebted to my family for supporting me through all my idiosyncrasies. I vowed to myself that I would always support them through their challenges in all ways I possibly could. Several opportunities arose for me to do just that.

Megan was preparing for her tenth grade examinations. She was very stressed and needed me as her stress-buster fluffy toy while she studied each night. I lay next to her and she used to recite her textbook material to me as if I understood!

It must have been the blurry look in my eyes that encouraged her to keep doing this each night. I was listening to physics, chemistry, biology, literature, history – I must admit a tad too much for my small little cerebral capacity! She would jokingly tell me I would be a scholar in my next life! I was delighted it helped Megan get over her stress, and beyond that excel in her examinations. I got a lot of recognition that I really did not understand.

Then came Angel – she sustained a fall while playing at a neighbour's place. She slipped in a puddle of water and broke her fall with a split at the entrance to the neighbour's home! It turned out to be a traumatic fall that fateful evening! Mummy was on an aircraft on one of her official trips and Daddy was in a business meeting! I heard Angel scream and cry so loud and she just could not get up! It was unmistakably Angel, my sister Angel! I had to alert the family! I began barking and running to the gate and then ran up to Megan's room to alert her as she was taking a nap after a hectic day at school! Megan sprang up, and so began a series of important events!

An ambulance arrived, and took Angel to the children's hospital. Angel underwent a serious emergency surgery as she had broken her left femoral shaft! The entire family was in a panic-stricken state over the next week. I never saw Angel until she returned from hospital with Mummy a week later! She was completely wheelchair bound and Mummy was taking care of her like a little baby for the next four months! I could not eat until I saw Angel and showed her and my family how attached I had grown to them. When Angel returned, Mummy and Angel spent their next four months on the ground floor as Angel could not negotiate the staircase until she was fully healed. I decided to stay with them on the ground floor all the time. I also understood that I should not climb onto Angel or her wheelchair. Angel was so touched by my care and love and she kept telling me how I had contributed to her speedy recovery. Again, I did not understand my contribution but felt happy I had helped in some way.

The saddest day of our lives was when our beloved Grandmother passed away suddenly while on a pilgrimage overseas.

She had bid farewell to us all just three days ago and left so energetically on her ten day trip. She had patted me specially and asked me what I may like as a gift when she returned. Now, I just wanted her back as I saw my family weeping uncontrollably at their loss. Like them, I too could not eat for days. She was a pillar in our family and loved us all in a very special way. I felt the loss as much as my family and joined them in prayer for Grandma to rest in peace. They kept telling each other and me that Grandma was our guardian angel looking after us all and I too believed that she was and is. My sisters and I often looked up at the brightest star in the sky believing that was Grandma! There was something magical about this and I gained strength every time I did this. Perhaps it was our beloved Grandma blessing us from above!

Months and years passed like this and I realised that I had such a symbiotic bond with my family. It was based on mutual love, respect and trust that grew day by day.

As I sat reminiscing my last seven years with my family, I counted my blessings for each happy moment.

Mine is a happy dog's life that is worth telling every dog and pet owner! It is a true celebration of life's small and large blessings!